MOMENTS OF LOVE

Paul Léautaud

MOMENTS
OF
LOVE

TRANSLATED BY AUSTRYN WAINHOUSE

THE MARLBORO PRESS

MARLBORO, VERMONT

1983

Manufactured in the United States of America.

Originally published in French as AMOURS.
© Editions Mercure de France 1965.

Library of Congress Cataloging in Publication Data

Léautaud, Paul, 1872-1956.
    Moments of love.

    Translation of: Amours.
    I. Title.
PQ263.E14A813   1983   843'.912   83-60468
ISBN 0-910395-06-3

Moments Of Love

Dormez, dormez
mes chères amours . . .

I LOVED FOR the first time in 1888. It was at year's end, and at Courbevoie. For about a year I had been working in Paris, taking the train every morning and not getting back until suppertime. I was becoming a young man. The mended trousers episode I have already written about* was well behind me. I was a bit more presentable by now, although still not yet a dandy. With my future stepmother away on another artistic tour, I was also a bit more at ease. In the house I had set up a little nook for myself, with a table for writing and some books. No ideas about literature as yet, however. Indeed, I believe I can say I had no ideas of any sort. But I did like being alone in this nook of mine whenever I could, that is, in the evening before going to bed, and on Sundays, when I did not have to go to Paris. I also liked my freedom, very extensive by now, my father never objecting to my going out whenever and for as long as I wished. When I was ten he was already telling me just to be sure to take a key: "Provided you come back home, that's all that matters." But Courbevoie!

---

* See appended notes, p. 89 ff.

Gone were the fine days of the Rue des Martyrs;* this town held no attraction for me, and I went out very seldom. Not much of a mixer to begin with, feeling no need of society at all, in this the same as I had been as a child, I had little companionship during my comings and goings between Paris and Courbevoie, and it was almost always glowering in a corner of the compartment that I traveled to my job and back from it. And who were the possible companions I was denying myself? My former classmates, at present office clerks like me, a pack of churls, interested only in playing cards during the whole trip, more loud-mouthed the one than the other. They'd never much liked me, precisely because I was withdrawn, and against them I had always felt defenseless because of my shyness. They really weren't my sort, and I did my utmost to keep out of their way. And I didn't always succeed, especially later on, after my military service, when I had returned to live at my father's and had begun to work in Paris again. I had a few nice mornings then, with the whole yelping pack pursuing me along the Boulévard Haussmann from where the Rue Auber crosses it to the Chaussée d'Antin. Quite without cause, naturally. Not knowing them, I paid no attention to them, that's all. Just think if one had to know all the people one had sat in a classroom with, or with whom one had been in the army! Why not all those one had ridden on a bus with? Such an attitude is what simple people, who enjoy rubbing elbows and whatnot, call putting on airs, apparently. Upon several occasions I saw one or another of those louts, on the Sunday visits I made now and then to Courbevoie during the last years my father was alive. They could all but bump straight into me, not one recognized me; but I recognized them. And for this I claim no credit. That imbecile manner, the one I had observed in them as raw youths, now that they were grown men more than ever distinguished their entire person.

It was in the course of those daily trips that I made the acquaintance of Léon Ambert, the brother of my first mistress. Actually, I had got to know him a little before then: that went back to my final months in school. He was the friend of a chum of mine named Chalgrain, and would often come to join him when we were let out at four o'clock. I can still see him, as I perceived him then, from afar, within the perspective of the Rue de la Garenne, an enormous dog beside him, a whip in his hand, speaking loudly, laughing loudly, gesticulating, cracking his whip, eyeing everybody with insolence. He lived on the Rue de la Station, a street that parallels the railroad and is intersected by the Rue de la Garenne, which goes underneath the tracks through a little tunnel; and on those afternoons when he came to get Chalgrain they'd walk together to the angle those two streets made. It was the end of summer. Without seeming to, I would contrive to trail them, walking a short distance behind, so as to watch Ambert fill the whole street with his voice and his movements. When they reached the corner of the Rue de la Station I would often see them joined by a pretty girl with golden hair, with a tinkling laugh, in a dress cut rather low both at the back of the neck and the front, and who seemed to have come to meet them. Chalgrain and Ambert would say goodbye, and Ambert would return into the Rue de la Station with the pretty girl while I kept straight on, heading in another direction. Had anyone told me then. . . .

Léon Ambert was just a year older than I, and was a student at the Ecole des Arts Décoratifs, in the sculpture department. And what a charming fellow already, so decorative himself and only too aware of it, with his pretty hair in curls over his forehead like a woman, his curled-up moustache, all his affected manners and his artistic look and bounce. At the age when one begins to use one's eyes he had already seen everything, he knew everything and was perfectly unselfish about it, indeed never happier than when he thought he was dazzling the person he had listening to him. For the rest, a heart as sensitive as they come, and a model friend, who always found the means to make use of you as well as to do you a favor from time to time, just for the pleasure of continually reminding you of it afterward. To those excellences one should perhaps add the Devil's own vanity, and an already very pronounced womanizing side behind which an equally flawless absence of scruple was developing, although all that was so natural to him one tended to lose sight of it. He was still only eighteen, but if his word meant anything, no woman resisted him, and the number of his mistresses was already very large. After that came the chapter on his family, artists all, and all outstanding, then the chapter on art and on his talent. Ah, the countless speeches on art I was treated to. I do believe that my enduring aversion for that word is owing as much to him as to the makers of fancy chocolates or of literary chinoiseries. That, he must have said to himself, that is devotion for you, he an artist! and I a petty clerk, but never mind, and he would talk to me about art anyhow. I see him yet, I hear him yet, unfolding theories without let, citing me names of artists and of works, sculptors and sculptures, with, naturally, thumb straight upraised, his other fingers clenched, modeling incomprehensible forms in empty space. What quivering of pride, what airs of assurance, what contentedness when next he spoke to me of what *he* wanted to do, of what he *would* do! How happy his mother would be then, his mother, such an admirable woman, as he used to tell me incessantly, making a tremendous display of his veneration for her, and proving once again that people with mothers invariably misuse them. However, where you really had to see him was on the chapter of honor. Honor, his word of honor—should I perhaps write it with a capital *h?*—that was this lad's strongest point of all. He talked to you about it all the time, tirelessly, in the most futile connections and in the gravest alike, and you were not supposed to laugh, or even smile. The bare idea of the faintest breach of honor roused his indignation, and the

13

hypothesis of a duel would instantly occur to him if you betrayed the least hint of disbelief. Impressive manifestations of a soul immersed in the ideal. Hearing him, your thoughts would stray off to those paladins of old, for whom honor outweighed very life itself. Unfortunately, ours has ceased to be an age for virtues of that magnitude. So keen a sense of honor was bound not to be understood, and Ambert was to discover this for himself a few years later, towards the middle of 1896. Having found a partner, he had set himself up as a photographer, and some toying with the bookkeeping then landed him in court, while his business associate, ruined and not liking it, blew his brains out. What a day that must have been, I mean for Ambert! True, he came through it unscathed, thanks to the protections obtained by his adoring mistress at the time, a young tart of forty, about whom I plan to say more by and by. But good Lord, so many moving protestations, so many fine phrases, hand over heart and eyes cast up to heaven! Gone, all gone with the little wind of a bullet. When I think that he was able to survive that disappointment! His sense of honor must have stood him in wonderful stead that day.

But these compliments are premature, at least within the chronological frame of these remembrances, and I return to my acquaintance with Ambert which quickly ripened into great friendship one for the other. A friendship whose grounds were so very self-evident, moreover. With me, Ambert could talk, rant, score points at will. Not very self-assured, by no means loquacious, capable of listening to him for hours—to him or to another—without opening my mouth, it didn't enter my head to contradict him or question his righteousness. Nor was I the way I am today, instantly alive to the qualities in people, driven by an irresistible urge to speak well of them. Defects and qualities, I reacted to them in about the same way, paying no special attention to either. I lived, I observed, I listened, acutely conscious of everything and retaining everything. For the rest, the world was going to have to wait; and, as they say, no one lost anything thereby. On my side, how could I help but be taken by Ambert, charming towards me, a true boon companion, always merry, amused and amusing: a complete change, as much from my family living room as from my customary young idiots. The charm of the *canaille,* as a spiteful tongue might have it. Gracious! Everyone to his taste. Your standard honest sort of person is so stupid, generally, and Ambert, underneath all his show, wasn't stupid at all. Nor were the good hours we spent together then, and the good outings, he ever deeper into his make-believe, and I so happy to stroll about, to feel free, to see things, to forget the suburbs I lived in, to wander around parts of the city that were unknown to me. I was working then at number 1 Rue d'Amboise for La Nation, an insurance company now defunct. I was on the mezzanine, in a little office whose windows looked out upon the street, and from where I could see reflections, shining in windowpanes across the way, of the huge iron safes at Fichet, Incorporated, located in those days at the corner of the Rue de Richelieu and the Rue d'Amboise. That little office, I think, is where I began my observations of the colleagues I had at my various jobs. Working with me there, first of all, was a very distinguished old gentleman named Rossi, an Italian, whose good mornings and goodbyes were always in the form of "Buon giorno, mio caro" and "A rivederci, signor!" and who from time to time swore a "Cazzo di Cristo!" when his figures weren't going right. Then a sort of mild-mannered, useless tatterdemalion named Ternaux, forever late, forever cheerful, and whose entire performance consisted in sleeping all day long on piles of policies heaped in front of him. The supervisor would wake him ever and anon. "How now, Monsieur Ternaux, what are you about?" "I, Sir? I'm waiting for six o'clock," Ternaux would reply, yawning. Then another one named Lerouxel de la Vionnière, an impecunious nobleman, who was in the habit of writing with enormous cork penholders. He was missing a finger on the right hand, which caused me uneasiness every time I had to shake hands with him. But the best was our office supervisor, Monsieur Delorme, a hefty open-faced fellow, straightforward, a former cavalry officer, one time rake, and who used now and then to rummage through his memories of past good fortune, he tipped back in his chair, we listening to him with deference, all of us smoking like chimneys. When we had fine weather and nothing urgent to attend to, he would send us out one by one to stretch our legs, or to listen to the band at the Palais Royal for an hour. For my part, I got special treatment. When Monsieur Delorme saw me having trouble getting started in the morning, head turned toward the window, eyeing the sunshine and the street, he knew what it meant: "Ah, ha, Monsieur Léautaud, you're itching to get over to the Latin Quarter. Very well, off with you. Come back after lunch." I needed no further invitation, I'd be out as fast as my nimble young legs could carry me. Sometimes I did not even come in, or didn't appear until eleven o'clock, having let Ambert lead me astray directly we pulled into the Gare Saint Lazare. It sufficed that I ask Monsieur Delorme to forgive me, which he would do with a smile. All sorts of things remind me of Monsieur Delorme, who has surely forgotten me after all this time. Every now and then I catch sight of him in Paris, on foot regardless of the weather, looking not very prosperous, and greying. I think of what a blow it must have been for him when La Nation folded. To find a job—and a job like the one he'd had—at his age, with a wife and child! How I'd enjoy stopping him and shaking hands. "Good day, Monsieur Delorme. You don't recognize me? Léautaud, you remember, don't you, Léautaud at La Nation?" But what would I say to him after that? And he always seems in a hurry. I have several times looked straight into his face, he has looked at me too, but he has never acknowledged me. Someday, however, I must do it. I certainly owe him that.

But to return to my relations with Ambert at this early stage. Arriving together in Paris in the morning, at the station we would meet up with one of his schoolmates, Sonnette, also a sculptor, and instead of going to my office I would set off with them. First we'd make a brief stop at the Ecole des Arts Décoratifs, where Ambert and Sonnette would shift some lumps of clay more or less about, or attend half a lecture, then we would nip along to the Musée du Luxembourg, to contemplate masterpieces, or to sit in the Gardens, or to make vast tours through that region extending from the Rue Monge to the Rue de Rennes, from the Seine up to the Boulévard Montparnasse. Those were my first venturings upon the Left Bank and all those districts seemed to me miles from anywhere. Like true friends, Ambert and Sonnette did their utmost to whip me into shape and to provide my artistic education too. I was in such need of one, and they were, along with being such pranksters, such connoisseurs already! A sheer waste of effort, however. I lacked the sacred fire. I was willing enough to accompany them wherever they went, watch what they did, roar with laughter at their college boy practical jokes, old as the hills. But that was all; an active role didn't interest me. I was equally unfit for serious things, like elevating my spirit to the pure summits of art. I recall our visits to the Musée du Luxembourg, and my first encounters with the *Olympia*. That picture, that painting, would elicit gales of laughter and abuse of all sorts from Ambert and Sonnette. "Now wouldn't you call that ugly, huh? And ridiculous?" they would say each time in an encouraging tone. Ugly? Ridiculous? There I would be all by myself, looking, while they were whooping it up. I'll not claim that I already saw all the beauty of *Olympia,* nor that I understood much, but why my two artists were laughing I understood not at all. We moved next to the works they admired, some Falguière nymphs or goddesses, sculptures by some Aimé Morot or other, a big painting by Bouguereau, titled, I believe, *Mater dolorosa,* and a few others of the same type that I've forgotten. And now what praise, what emotion! Their two souls attained communion in genius, neither more nor less. As for me, I'd wait, in silence, as always, resolutely inaccessible to beautiful things despite the thorough tutoring I'd received. The feeling for art, 'tis a mysterious thing. Ambert has ended up a strolling player working the provinces, and Sonnette today sculpts the façades of houses. I alone am still what I was, I have even clung to my failings, as in the days when *Olympia* somehow captivated me and when so many masterpieces left me cold.

That is where the advantages I derived from Ambert's friendship remained for some time. I knew that he together with his mother and his sister lived in the house of an uncle, his mother's brother, an outstanding engineer, I'd been told. Everything connected with Ambert was of such premium quality! Rue de la Station was the location, a detached building surrounded by a garden. Each morning, when the train we were on passed their house, he would point to his mother, that admirable woman, who was waving goodbye to him, standing in the doorway of a kitchen, surrounded by a halo of saucepans. Sometimes too his sister appeared at a window—the first one on the right, second story—still scarcely dressed, and she too would make a little sign to him. It was the pretty golden-haired girl I'd seen before. His father had left his mother a long time ago, when he and his sister were small children. His father was the son of an opera singer who had had a certain popularity in his day, and the brother of two singers in comic opera, one of whom, it seemed, had attained true celebrity. Ambert's father in his youth had himself dreamt of the same career, he too possessing a very fine voice and amazing gifts, naturally, but adverse luck, the stupidity of having married, the ensuing children ... etc. So many glories to which Ambert drew my attention all the time, assuring me he would not fail to confirm them some day, just wait. So I knew all that, and that's all there was to it until one Sunday, as my father had forgotten to turn in his theater pass, the idea came to me to give Ambert a treat. I asked my father for his pass, and I dashed off to propose to my friend that he use it to go that same evening to the Comédie Française. Ambert must have talked about me, and had probably, out of habit, attributed merits to me by the handful, and they must have been fully prepared to see me, for I was given a grand welcome. In less than an hour I became acquainted with the uncle, with his wife, with their granddaughter, and with their son, who was about my own age. There was also Ambert's grandmother, very much the old-fashioned elderly lady and positively mindless, then his mother, an excellent good-natured woman, huge, and very simple of mind, somewhat the unsuspecting old lady who becomes the victim in horror dramas, finally Mademoiselle Jeanne, a self-possessed young lady, who seemed to have everybody eating out of her hand and who filled the whole house with her laughter, her voice, and the brightness of her golden hair. The pass was accepted with pleasure, and I left, laden with invitations to come back without standing on ceremony, whenever I chose, as often as I wanted.

This is a fine occasion to say something that applies throughout this entire story. I have always been in my relationships the same as I am when in love. I have never strained myself, I have never sought to be more loving or loveable than is normal for me. The world is such a queer place, however, that I have always won, and rather decisively won, the sympathy of those I have let come close to me. This again and again leaves me amazed in the extreme, it having come about with so little thought on my part, and so little effort. Yet another person who adores me, I say to myself, much affected; we'll see how long it lasts. And naturally I never see the end of it, so true it is that habit is a second nature. On the other hand, people who have set eyes on me but once or twice, or only fleetingly, those ones are hard to please, find me blunt, disagreeable, unsociable, in short not worth having anything to do with. Might I cite the example of my mother, who had to do with me for eight days all told in her life? No way of making myself appreciated, not with her, and each time we saw one another it was only to wait longer before seeing one another again. The extraordinary phenomenon was repeated in all its phases at the house of Ambert's uncle. The more I went there, the more I was asked to come back, and by my fifth visit I was already considered a member of the household. Furthermore, I was quite right in thinking, the first time, that they knew a bit about me before I got there. It seemed that I already had quite a little reputation in Courbevoie. My father's house was imagined to be the scene of every depravity, he passed for a man who had droves of women permanently in his bed, and I myself was thought to sleep in earnest with all the maids. In earnest! when in actual fact that was still so far from the case. Unfortunately, they had also heard about my struggles with my future stepmother, the *dolce vita* I was just emerging from. That attenuated my legend, they believed less in my escapades. Soon, indeed, they beheld them as so much tittletattle, and I appeared in my natural colors, divested of all prowesses. As of the Sunday when I went to give Ambert the theater pass, and even before I began my affair with his sister, I do believe I spent all my Sundays in that house. Everybody, down to the uncle's four-year-old granddaughter, who clamored for me the whole week, would be so thrilled to see me. I used to arrive towards two o'clock, and would mingle with the visitors who happened to be there. Ambert's uncle, the remarkable engineer, would be explaining his research, in which each took what interest he could. I also recall the Sunday when a head of Mercury sculpted by Ambert was put up over the front door of the house. The piece is still there, although different tenants took the house over long ago, and when I was still making occasional trips to Courbevoie while my father was alive, I'd gaze at it every time the train took me past. Then, the visitors gone, we'd dine, one great happy family, I admirably placed between the two young ladies of the house, the little one and the grown up, and afterward we'd remain chatting until about eleven. What on earth could I have said and recounted, for my part? Damned if I remember! I just let myself be adored, and there you have it.

First moments of love, which leave such indelible memories behind! I try to recollect how my amours with Jeanne Ambert got started, and can you imagine, my mind is a blank. It must have begun two or three months after I was admitted into the house, perhaps less. Looking back upon any such happiness one easily overestimates its time in coming. As I said, she was very free-spirited, even boylike in her behavior, and we became good friends right away. I provided a change from the solemn people she was surrounded by. No need, with me, to be sober, to behave with dignity, things that bored her to tears. To the contrary, the more improperly she behaved, the more she touched my heart. She would join in the games I played with the uncle's little granddaughter, and often I found myself, without expecting it, hiding with her in the same spot while the child hunted for us. Ah, the games that love and intention play together. I in those days was truly the last thing from the wily seducer, and it was indeed she who began, or at least encouraged me, by creating the circumstances. She was, besides, so much more venturesome than I. And there was her age, too. She is five years my elder, I was seventeen, she was therefore twenty-two. A young woman, that is, both in temperament and in her underlying sense of management. In addition, she was much taken with me, and she was open enough about it, even too open, as I was to find out later when her mother told me some little things pertaining to this period. At any rate, I met with no difficulty, we had both been heading in the same direction, she still more quickly than I, and had been waiting for quite some time when I finally started in. As to attempting her portrait, I don't know what to say. Imagine a tall girl, of a very unusual presence, and as a woman voluptuousness itself, one of those women every man turns and looks at, with the skin and glow redheads have when they are pretty. Without undue boastfulness I may interject here that up until now I have had rather pretty girls. I have some photographs of Jeanne, taken at points scattered throughout the period her beauty lasted, perhaps ten years at the outside. Someday, can one ever tell? when the last of us has moved out, those portraits will perhaps be discovered along with those of all the people figuring in my memoirs, and published. Then shall they see whether I have spoken true. A pretty woman for a mother, a pretty girl for a first mistress! That sometimes adorns your daydreams for a lifetime. As I said before, I am still trying to recall the beginning of our affair and I still find nothing definite, other than this. I had gone to Paris one Sunday afternoon. It was understood that I would be back for supper at Rue de la Station. When I returned she was on the doorstep. I had bought a bouquet of violets for her. Finding her there, all alone, in the descending dusk, I gave her the flowers. She pretended to be surprised, I remember that, and I must have said to her, with my customary amiableness, the sweet words she was waiting for and which she had done everything to bring forth.

After that, what a romance, due certainly to require a good many pages from me, without counting the cost in emotion. At the Rue de la Station I was a familiar sight, not just on Sunday, but nearly every evening as well. Jeanne was so skillful at prompting everybody to send for me, and I had such reasons for answering the summons! Was she not my whole life, this pretty girl? at least that is what I told myself, soundly convinced of it. I spent every week-day impatiently waiting for the moment when I would see her in the evening, and all week yearning for the blissful Sunday; and she did the same. It can only have been the rarest luck that the uncle's and aunt's suspicions weren't roused sooner. Jeanne steered the whole business, indeed, I left everything in her hands. When I turned up on Sunday I was not seen to tarry in the uncle's study, listening to him descant upon his employments. Those great questions did not interest me anymore, I much preferred to go off with Jeanne to another room, in the negligible company of her mother and grandmother. There, we'd frisk about, we'd chatter, we'd give ourselves over to being in love. There was a music box, we'd have it going a great deal. *La Gavotte Stéphanie,* Weber's *Dernière Pensée, La Promenade sur l'eau,* and still other tunes whose names have not stuck with me, they'd be rattled off one after another, heightened by the scrape of toiling metal. Oh, it was charming. At this period Jeanne gave me a picture of herself, a photograph, the first I had from her, and I have it still. This photograph dated back a little, to the time when she was seventeen or eighteen and still living on Rue Lamarck, where she was born, and in it she was a little puffy, with masses of hair tumbling down over her brow, as was yet stylish, but even so, how that picture delighted me. On the back she had written a dedication: "From his beloved to her dearest Paul. Given the 14th day of April 1889. Love and Fidelity. Jane." The 14th of April, 1889! Seventeen! Ah, youth! When I reread those adorable lines, I find them as foolish as an epitaph on a tombstone. Inspired by love, I too used to take flight, true enough. I had quit my Paris job—one witty remark too many addressed to La Nation's head accountant—and I had found something temporarily, there in Courbevoie, at a small local newspaper where I had nothing to do. There I remember writing for my idol a few of those verses whereof the songs of Monsieur Xavier Privas would give a fair idea, were they not even more ridiculous. Fortunately, my timidity on this subject saved me, and she for whom they were intended never knew anything about these masterpieces, anymore than I myself know what I did with them. At any rate, that poetic interlude was very brief. I soon found another job in Paris, at 11 Rue de la Grange Batelière, with a kind of swindler, and my commutings with Ambert resumed. How everybody would stand to gain if every girl had a brother like that! My affair with his sister had further strengthened the ties between us. As they had no secrets from each other, she had put him wise the very first day, in so doing reminding him that she was his elder and that he had nothing to say to anybody. That indeed was an injustice to him, to that noble heart. Ambert was too beholden to his sister on his own account for him to say anything whatever; instead, he did his best to aid us. For example, he acted as courier for the letters Jeanne and I exchanged, seeing each other every day not being enough. People have so much to say to each other when in love, including things so sacred they can only be written! The son's friendship, so great, the daughter's love, so pleasing, had in addition earned me the kindnesses of their mother, admirable enough all right, so I was beginning to believe. Every morning I set

out from home well before the train was due, and went
to pick up Ambert at his house. Nobody would be up
except himself and his mother, ever on hand to coddle
him. Breakfast would be ready, cosy as could be. I'd
have my share, then we'd leave together. When the
train taking us to Paris went past, no more jealous feelings; each of us had his little greeting from afar, I one
from Jeanne, who jumped out of bed and ran to her
window just to wave to me, and he a wave from his
mother. And again, when I returned in the evening, I'd
take an indirect route home, by way of the Rue de la
Station. Jeanne would be waiting for me on the doorstep, affectionate, full of appeal, and we would remain
there together for a few minutes while Ambert kept the
family distracted inside, or walked the dog along the
railroad embankment, talking and laughing noisily so
that nobody might get the idea to come and look. I do
not wish to forget, either, the evening activities at their
uncle's house, with which those days frequently con-
cluded. Further hours of delight! I would come for dinner, or else would arrive afterward. The uncle would
shut himself up in his study. Ambert was usually absent,
gone again to Paris on an errand, or to play the young
spark. Seated around a big table in the dining room, we
were only the uncle's wife and her son, the grandmother
and the mother of Ambert, and Jeanne and myself. We
drank tea, we talked, we played lotto. Ah, the first
squeezings of the beloved's hand ... Jeanne always sat
next to me, and the lotto once under way she

would slide a hand beneath the table (. . . . . .) and remain thus (. . . . . .) throughout the game. She had hit
upon that all by herself, the precious angel, and how
well inspired she was. From time to time she would
pause to regain countenance, then back to it she would
come. I can still hear her laughing over the complete
unawareness of the others, poring over their cards.
Those good people did not indeed suspect a thing; but
what if they had discovered us! Me especially; wouldn't I
have cut a pretty figure? But the grandmother who
could scarcely see, the mother who was blind in another
sense, with a son and daughter who did whatever they
pleased, and the uncle's son who didn't care a fig anyhow—what danger was there of our being discovered?
Even had they seen us, what on earth could they have
said? As for the aunt, Jeanne always contrived to have us
seated well away from her. I also clearly remember one
evening before dinner, in the anteroom. Everyone was
proceeding from the uncle's study toward the dining
room. We were last. Jeanne then went forth into the
unlighted anteroom, halted in a kind of corner by the
stairway. Then I walked out, and was about to go by
without seeing her when she caught my arm and drew
me near to kiss me, and there, the next minute (. . . . . . .
. . . .) Another evening I
had simply come to the door to give her a kiss as usual.
She took my hand, led me into the garden and round to
the rear. The house was divided on the ground floor by
a hallway which formed the anteroom I spoke of, with

two exterior doors, one at the front, the other to the garden in back. She led me in quietly by that back door, down the hallway, then up the little stairway to the second floor, and into her room. It was my first time there. There was no light. Downstairs, the whole family was at dinner, as peaceful as so many Baptists. Jeanne went back down, ate a quick bite, then rejoined me. Here we were, truly alone for the first time, she surrendered in my arms, my hands, underneath her dressing-gown, touching her almost naked body. Delightful, unforgettable moment, and what an opportunity! She had certainly expected great things from this clandestine encounter, had my lovely friend. Her bed was right there. We even sat down upon it, if I am not mistaken. But I was unsure, my mind was on other things, just what was wrong with me I no longer know—did I perhaps feel unsafe?—and all we did was kiss. I stayed there about an hour; then, a moment having come when the coast was clear, I left the same way, Jeanne guiding me in the dark, both of us on tiptoe. In retrospect it goes down as one more misfire, or the next thing to it.

We also carried on out of doors, now and then, and shortly we shall see that if Ambert put all his friendship into backing our cause, it sometimes brought him dividends. At that time in Courbevoie, on the Rue de Normandie, two steps from where my father lived, in a rather secluded little house in this as yet not very built up area, there was a Madame Lefébure, and she had two daughters, one in her twenties, the other thirteen or

fourteen years old. Thither all the young fops of Courbevoie did hie themselves every evening, to dance atten-
dance upon the mother and elder daughter, while the
younger served in the capacity roughly of a maid. Madame Lefébure was still youthful, and appeared even
more so, at a slight distance, admittedly, thanks to her
girlish costumes and little googoo simperings, and beside her daughter, the one no less skinny, no less dolled
up, and of no less risqué demeanor than the other, the
difference was not very great. Both more or less exhibited themselves at the amateur concerts given at Courbevoie each year. I remember having seen them there
once or twice, clumsy, inane, with voices like canvas
ripping, in comic songs befitting their abilities. Shades,
it seemed to me, of my future stepmother, in the days
when she exhibited herself likewise and with like glitter,
in similar concerts. As for Monsieur Lefébure, the husband and father, he was a man who got in nobody's
way. He was a traveling salesman, it seems, or something of the sort. Each month he made an appearance
before his wife, in the middle of the night, then took
himself away at dawn to resume his itinerant existence.
At any rate it was under those colors the mother and
daughter presented him to their young suitors, who
were numerous, I repeat. Think of it! two actresses, and
neither one of them overly shy, the charm of talent and
the allure of easy thighs; failing the daughter, the
mother; or failing the mother, the daughter; even sup-
posing it wasn't both at once! For those young blades it

was something of a high old time, and not expensive, and the house was always full, often until very late in the night. Now, Ambert would not have been Ambert if he had not endeavored to practice his young lady-killing talents there too. Which of the two he courted, the mother or the daughter, I never found out. My guess is that he wouldn't have cared. Doubtless all he was after was to have one of them, in order to be able to brag about it afterward, and he must certainly have courted both at once. Furthermore, seductive as he was and knowing so well how to talk to women and how to go about it with them, both would leap into his arms, he was perfectly sure of it. The one difficulty facing him was to find the way of going there every night, until victory was achieved. For, annoyingly enough, evenings, precisely, were when he was least free, his uncle disliking having him outside after supper. Were he to want to go to Paris for the evening, he could claim it was to attend a lecture, that went down pretty well. But for going out right there in Courbevoie what excuse could he find, and use several evenings in a row? My ongoing amours with his sister soon gave him an idea. Springtime was beginning. One could already consider taking an after-supper stroll: an excellent motive for going out. All that remained was to confer with Jeanne. Brother and sister going out together, there'd certainly be no objections to that. So he conferred with Jeanne. Wouldn't she be tickled to take a little stroll with me, while he went to lay his heart before the Rue de Normandie ladies? Quite as he anticipated, she agreed at once, and the excursions were organized. Almost every evening for a good fortnight, supper once over, Jeanne or Ambert would talk vaguely about taking a walk, just stepping out briefly for a bit of air. The other would say yes right away, or else would feign reluctance and then finally give in, as if to please Uncle, who found those goings on so natural that he was the first to encourage them, even prodding whichever of the two was playing lazybones, and at length they would both set out, arm in arm, seeming in no more of a hurry than if they were going nowhere. We would meet on a streetcorner; and Ambert would tear off to his women while Jeanne and I struck out for the lovely countryside around Courbevoie, continuing well beyond the last houses, most often along the railroad tracks, past a highway called the Le Havre Road. Having found a quiet spot, and a suitable place to sit down, we would stay there for half an hour, an hour, depending upon how much time we had, and give ourselves over wholeheartedly to the caresses, to the enchanting games that we practiced underneath the table during those evenings at her uncle's. Here, with plenty of room for maneuver, my trousers were soon unbuttoned, her skirts soon raised. Yet, throughout, what scrupulous purity—relative, if you wish. We mutually allowed ourselves some rather lively onanism, nothing more. I no longer have a very distinct memory of those moments, at any rate of my sensations during them. Our two imaginations put together probably went no farther than these games, or else I must not have dared and she, despite strong inclinations, must have hesitated to go ahead. One of those outings remained particularly vivid. That evening we had gone in a different direction, and were sitting in a little wood, called the Bois de Kilford, on Rue de Kilford, a stones-throw from her uncle's house, just on the other side of the railroad embankment. Even in broad daylight no one could have seen us, so snugly were we hidden within a little thicket. I caressed her and I took her in my arms (. . . . .) Wonderful, wonderful walks that we took, when our young hearts beat so in unison. Afterwards, at the place agreed upon, we would be joined by Ambert, and he and Jeanne would then return home together, as nice as you please, like a good brother and sister back from their constitutional.

Ambert, of course, was more the gallant than I. Not only was he already making love in earnest—and that certainly was the way to do it—while I lagged far behind, but he was doing it in several places, and the Lefébure ladies were not causing him to neglect his Paris friends. Apropos of these he unveiled this scheme one evening when the three of us were together: "I'd like to spend an evening in Paris with a woman I know and take her to the theater. Maybe, if you could, you'd get me tickets for the Comédie, bringing them to the house, making it look like an idea coming from you. I'll pretend Jeanne and I are going together, and we'll meet

34

you in Paris. Jeanne will stay with you all evening and I'll join the two of you after the show to take the train home." Ambert was charming with me, there's no disputing that. He was asking me to look after his sister for an evening while he spent a few hours with his girlfriend. I felt quite unable to refuse. So I accepted. Scrutinizing it now, the whole business—at this distance— has a questionable look, all right. Brother and sister must have been in cahoots. Indeed, may not that excellent scheme have first originated with Jeanne, may she not have won Ambert over to it, laying out before him all he would gain thereby? She must have been fully aware that you could get anything from him by pandering howsoever little to his interests. But how about honest love, pure love, love minus the loving? One does what one can. Even had they occurred to me, these moral stupidities would not have stopped me, of that I am sure. I was so accustomed to living in an equivocal atmosphere, throughout the entirety of my affair with Jeanne as amongst others who lived in the same way, without it ever disturbing me! True, I lived that way unthinkingly, there was my one error. But for that, I would today have one further pleasure as I look back upon the past.

And so I asked my father for a pair of tickets, and Ambert and I got busy preparing our rendezvous. As I have said, I was then working on Rue de la Grange Batelière, number 11. In that office, I recall in passing, one of my colleagues was a young journalist who had so ex-

tolled political economy to me and discovered in me
such aptitudes for it, that studying political economy
was all I talked about. Ambert's uncle, who saw in me a
potential orator, felt that political economy would be
the crowning touch. It was also while I was working in
that job that Ambert inveigled me into an operation
which could have caused me all sorts of trouble. He had
told me some story or other about needing fifty francs,
absolutely and without delay. For me, fifty francs was a
sum, and I was far from having it. Then I recalled that
in Courbevoie my father had a café owner, next to the
church, from whom he sometimes got a loan when he
was short of cash. Often I myself had run those errands
on his behalf. Lo! a solution. I submitted it to Ambert,
he so swore by all his gods that he'd have the money
when it was due that I wrote out a one-month I O U
the way my father did, and took it to the said publican,
who handed me the banknotes without looking at the
paper. Naturally, the day before the loan expired the
good Ambert hadn't yet rounded up the first penny, and
everything had to be paid the next day if my father was
not to find out about it. Ambert for his part was con-
tent to despair, without doing anything useful to get
me out of my fix, and perhaps at bottom not caring; but
my heart was in my boots. Then I had the idea of writing to my Godmother Bianca, whom I'd not seen in
years, ever since my old nanny left who used to take me
to her house on Sundays, delightful days that ended too
soon. I described the mess I was in, and the reply

was prompt. Her lady companion came to my office the next day; she gave me the fifty francs, and I was able to redeem the note that same evening and put an end to my nightmare. I was thoughtless enough to forget to write a letter of thanks, which almost spoiled our relations, to my great regret. But I come now to our evening in Paris. The day before I had gone to the Hotel des Martyrs, which stood at number 7 Rue des Martyrs. There too was the Brassérie des Martyrs that I had come to know in my childhood. The hotel I am speaking of disappeared a few years ago, and the entire building is now occupied by a draper's shop called La Galérie des Martyrs. I had reserved a room for the following evening, and arranged to have supper served there, paying for everything in advance, about twenty-five francs, I believe. Nor was I overcharged. Everything was fine. At six o'clock Ambert arrived at my office with Jeanne and, placing her in my safekeeping, dashed off to his rendezvous while we made a dash for the Rue des Martys. Has Jeanne sometimes thought of the party we had together in that attractive hotel-room, hung in blue throughout, such a feminine room, and still in all its details so vividly remembered by me! did she used to think of it when she lived in the neighborhood with her husband, around 1900–1902? It constitutes a splendid memory, especially for a first tryst. Despite our handsome arrangements, that evening I was once again as I had been with the maid I have spoken of:* the same lack of know-how and of enterprise. The two episodes were so close in time, moreover; a matter of a few months at most. Jeanne too had enormous inhibitions, which with each attempt produced more fear in her than pleasure, so that we confined ourselves to our customary exercizes, on a bigger scale; and that was all. And, besides, the time had flown by so quickly. Soon it was eleven o'clock, and time to get up and get dressed and get back to our suburb. I can still see Jeanne, as we were about to go, rounding up all the candles left over from the ceremony, for the reading she always did in her room, she said, when all lights were out. We had decided to meet on the Place de la Trinité, at a little café that is still at the Chausée d'Antin corner. We found Ambert already there and waiting for us, and so we all three went straight to the station. On the platform I ran into my father, also returning home; Ambert and his sister introduced to him, we all boarded the train together. To Ambert alone was destined all the pleasure of that ride. Seated opposite my father, he never stopped talking the whole while it lasted. A theater personality! What an occasion to sparkle! All the forebears were trundled out, the opera singer grandfather, the pair of comic opera singing aunts, the engineer uncle and the admirable mother, after which came his, Ambert's, own qualities, his own talents, and his own future glory. My father was always of an excellent humor, with others. Why yes, he had known the two singers very well, actually. He chatted most cordially with Ambert. As for Jeanne and myself, we laughed at the appropriate moments but spoke little, just the amount politeness required. Was she perhaps thinking about her party, about how, her party notwithstanding, she was just where she had been before it, the poor darling? As for me, I was probably preoccupied by something graver still. Weren't we going to have to leave each other until the morrow? How cruel the slightest separation becomes when you are in love! Everybody has been through that, no need to labor the point.

It was a little after the Hotel des Martyrs soirée that I began my employment at *La République française,* 42 Rue de la Chausée d'Antin, a newspaper best left in its obscurity. Those, lest I am mistaken, were the final days of Boulangism.* At the paper I came into more or less close contact with some diversely famous people; it won't hurt if, after some selecting, I give a few of their names here. First of all, the man who was editor-in-chief at the time, Monsieur Joseph Reinach,* whose writings are all so amusing, and for whom I acted as secretary several times. Then Jules Ferry,* whom I can still see climbing the stairs to the editorial office, round-shouldered, his expression apprehensive, his glance sidewise, seemingly in perpetual dread of I don't know what from behind. Next, Monsieur Eugène Pitou, editorial secretary, about whom the building concièrge was simply crazy, you could tell it from the way she would run out and plant herself in the courtyard, suddenly frozen into some statue of admiration whenever he passed by. And Madame Jeanne de la Vaudère, then making her debut

in the literary world with a novel that was being serial-
ized in the paper, and that I did not read, anymore than
I read any of those she published afterwards. Finally I
shall present Monsieur Friedmann, my cashier and office
chief, a tall, lean Alsatian, brusk and hot-tempered, but
underneath all that a great fellow. Like me, Monsieur
Friedmann lived in Courbevoie, he knew my father very
well, and knew all about the delightful life we had at
home. Switching now to the subject of home, my step-
mother-to-be had returned from her tour, the latest and
most fruitful one, bringing a child back with her, and
my pleasures had begun afresh. So had the gracious
speeches of times past, unseasonable now. But thus to
behold me going out every evening, heedless of her and
of her squawking, that was beyond her comprehension
and she picked every sort of quarrel with me. More re-
grettably, my father, with whom I had got on fairly well
while she was off spellbinding the boondocks, had gone
back to being against me ever since her return. This
shortly led to a first falling-out, the recital of which will
add to my collection of paternal anecdotes, so different,
I note without regret, from those of Monsieur Claretie.*
Every day, white bread and wholewheat bread, equal
amounts of each, were delivered to the house. The former was for the table, the latter for the dogs. But, my
father and my future stepmother being passionately
fond of that latter, everything was reversed. The wholewheat bread was kept for the table, it was the white
bread that was given to the dogs. Now, I wasn't in per-

fect agreement with my family on this score either. I for my part disliked wholewheat bread, and asked again and again that some of the other sort be set aside for me. What! to be treated like the dogs, wasn't that asking rather a lot? Naturally, these matters lying outside my father's domain, it was to his gracious companion that I addressed myself; but all she could find by way of reply—and couched in such exquisite terms!—was that if I was not satisfied, I had but to shove off, they'd be delighted if I did, my father foremost of all. No indeed, I was not satisfied, and on several counts; but as for shoving off, hold on there. That sort of talk would get her nowhere, I told her so straight out. This was my home as much as hers, and it had been mine first—I'd overheard my father employ that compelling formula during a scene they had over me—, if it was for anyone to tell me to leave, it wasn't she, and as for my father, the day he told me to, I'd be able to handle things without any help from her. That fine day arrived. Rather, that fine evening. He didn't have to go to the theater, and we were dining together. Such evenings, furthermore, were the only ones when I got a proper dinner. The other evenings, when he ate at six o'clock and then left for the Comédie, I would reach home to find the table cleared, and my future stepmother off socializing with neighborhood gossips, and I would make what shift I could. Anyhow, the good man was there, like the wholewheat bread, which was served to me yet once again. And this time, after all my entreaties, I put

41

my foot down, confessing my amazement at such obstinacy on their part. Whether because he was in a bad
mood or because his paramour had wound him up, my
behavior drove my father frantic, and that man driven
frantic was a sight worth seeing. "If you are not satisfied," said he, "you can go eat elsewhere and clear out!"
Just what the other one had said! Those two souls were
closely attuned indeed. There and then I resolved to
leave them to their happiness. Dinner over, they went
out for a walk about town, and I found myself alone. It
was sacrifice myself now or never. From the attic I carried down a small trunk that my father had used in former days when on tour. I packed my things into it and,
without worrying about the neighbors, locked the front
door and took the train to Paris. With around ten francs
in my pocket! In Paris I got into a cab, was driven to the
Rue Monsieur le Prince where I took a room in a hotel
chosen at random, the then Hotel de la Lozère, at present the Hotel des Charentes; with those people it's easy
come, easy go. Ah, that little home, adjoining the
water-closets, in that flophouse for students, and that
first evening of *home rule*. Not one of my cheerier memories. To live in such places, to think that some people
get used to them. I went back out at once, went off to
spend the rest of the evening brooding over things outside a wineshop that still forms the corner of the Rue
Monsieur le Prince and the Boulévard Saint Michel,
there where you have to go down some steps, and returned only in order to go to bed, as I did every night

while I lived in that hotel. At the office the following morning the first thing I did was apprise Monsieur Friedmann of my change of domicile and of the prologue to it. I had his immediate approval, backed up by an advance to keep me afloat. For two or three days I was in peace, then my father came to life. He began by writing to me, he who never wrote letters, and ordered me to return. Ordering, that was that man's forte. Understanding, less so. Next, he complained to Monsieur Friedmann about my having left. He was given a good reception. "My dear friend," the kindly Alsatian said to him, "I am on your son's side, and I'm not the only one. Even so, I'm willing to try to talk him into going home. But only upon one condition. You are going to promise not to say a word to him about his leaving or the money he has spent." Peace, it had been decreed, was not yet to be mine. In a burst of love for me, my father coughed up the promise. Monsieur Friedmann put his charm to work, and a week later I was welcomed back into my delightful family. But the spell was broken. The inevitable had only been postponed.

And over there on Rue de la Station, in the pavillion of my amours, the situation was not much better. The aunt, a dark-browed, unattractive little woman, was very envious of Jeanne; and as, apparently, she had finally realized what was going on between us, there was a rather spectacular blow-up. Madame Ambert, that good woman, had meant to straighten everything out, and had naturally made everything worse instead, the while

43

being taxed with inexcusable blindness. All that was recounted to me one evening while we were taking a
walk, Jeanne, Ambert, their mother and I, with recom-
mendations to show myself somewhat less often until
the dust had settled. For Ambert this was the proper occasion to expose to us the underlying reason behind his
aunt's fury, who had used my intimacies with Jeanne as
a pretext. The truth? The woman was mad about him, it
was fairly obvious, moreover, and had he wished to sleep
with her! But a boy like him—nothing doing! Whereupon Madame Ambert bent an affectionate gaze his
way, approving him with her best effort at a knowing
air. Soon the dissension in the house sharpened, with
everybody contributing to it, from the outraged aunt to
Ambert and Jeanne who saw nothing wrong in the idea
of becoming free; and, in the middle, the son of the
uncle, much amused by the whole thing. Rue de la
Station became an inferno, family life a memory, and
Madame Ambert had to resign herself to leaving
her remarkable brother and going to live in Paris
with her children. Another fine evening, the one
when I heard that piece of news. Despite its enormity,
Madame Ambert was all aflutter, while her children
went on steadily praising her decision, fearing lest she
change her mind. For three days there was no Ambert,
reported to be busy hunting for accomodations in the
vicinity of his school. Then all that remained was to
organize the moving, the mountain of packages, the
farewell ritual.

About here, I believe, is where one must put the get-together at which Jeanne and I retrieved our weak conduct in the Hotel des Martyrs. On second thought, it may not have taken place until after the departure from Courbevoie; but if so it was very soon after the setting up in Paris, and I am in error by only a few days. We had agreed to meet one afternoon at three o'clock on the square next to the Palais Royal, and the ceremony transpired, this time, in a room of the Hotel de Lisbonne, at number 4 Rue de Vaugirard, and I have the clearest recollection of what it looked like when I arrived there. And of the pretty demonstration I gave of my greenness. I remember how, as I showed the desk clerk a little briefcase I always dragged about with me, stocked with papers and books, I felt called upon to tell him I had come in order to do some work, and asked him to bring me up some writing materials, all that to camouflage my embarrassment. I ought indeed to have made a few notes, what's more, as since then I have always done, even in less solemn circumstances, like the death of my father, for example, or the interview with my mother in Calais. At least I would now have a few good lines to put down. For, would you believe it, my memories stop right here on that great day when with Jeanne, and for the first time, I made love in earnest. Searching would simply be to wear myself out for nothing. I reconstruct it all, that pale pink body, those full, firm breasts, that face shining from eagerness, other still more interesting beauties, I inhale that redhead odor, the odor emanating from hair and body; but the details, the pleasure, my own pleasure, my eagerness ... Not more than if it had been some other. The overexcitement inseparable from a first performance, perhaps?

Anyhow, the day came for the departure. That was in the earlier half of 1889, probably the end of May or beginning of June. A world's fair had opened not long before. Ambert, his mother and Jeanne installed themselves in a little apartment in a shabby building, miles away from my part of the city, way out in the Rue du Faubourg Saint Jacques, at number 13. When all that was done I was told about it, and I went to have a look. I still recall my impression of the distance which, the first time, seemed immense. From then on I spent all my Sundays there. I would set out early from Courbevoie, stop first at *La République française* for the Sunday mail, then head for the Faubourg Saint Jacques, either on foot or on the top deck of the Montparnasse-Place Saint Jacques omnibus, done away with in recent years. The house, now demolished, used to project a little beyond the building line, and once I reached the last houses on the Rue Saint Jacques I would perceive, far away, beyond the intersection with the Boulévard de Port Royal, at a window of the apartment, a beloved golden head (blonde, old style) on the look-out for my coming. It would be between nine and nine-thirty. Madame Ambert was off marketing, or starting out when I arrived. Jeanne would be wearing just that amount of clothes I liked, and thereupon, each time, we would have a pleas-

ant moment of intimacy, of loving, of youthfulness—
that's the word I wanted. Ah, how keen in me is the
memory of those mornings! I still feel it all, down to the
bright sun's warmth, and that's a pretty detail, isn't it?
Everything is so fine when, eyes gazing straight ahead,
you embark upon a whole lifetime! and one rumples so
quickly. After that it seldom amounts to anything more
than pulling the same trick off again, as best one can,
the unforeseen and the novelty being there no longer.
Since the departure from Courbevoie Ambert had prac-
tically ceased living under his mother's roof. Only rarely
did he come home for the night, or stop by to see her in
the daytime, to tell her how he was getting along. In
the very midst of the move, one day on the boulevard,
whether by chance, whether because he had been ac-
tively seeking him, he had run into his father. The son
of the opera singer, the brother of the two comic singers, himself once a candidate for a lyrical career, after
having spent some time in the soap manufacturing business, had simply become a retouch-man in a photographer's studio, and was spinning out his days in Levallois,
with a mistress by whom he had a son. The encounter
of the two artists had been very cordial. How family
feeling does keep, at a distance! The day after that meeting it was as though father and son had never been out
of each other's sight. Ambert, taken off to Levallois, had
made the acquaintance of his father's new family; and
the fare was so good and the lady so charming, that,
having been offered a room, he had put up no resistance

and was now genuinely established there, the pride and promise of the house. And his good fortune had good repercussions. It befell that one Sunday, I myself, having left Jeanne and her mother a little late, reached the Gare Saint Lazare too late to catch the last train, and found myself obliged to return to the Faubourg Saint Jacques. Her son's bed being available, Madame Ambert could not but propose it to me, and thus I slept in her house for the first time. After that fine first step the rest was speedily accomplished. From then on, instead of coming only on Sunday morning, I began to show up as of Saturday afternoon, right after I finished at the office, and to stay on until I returned to the office on Monday morning. Thus I got there sooner, and on Sunday morning Jeanne and I were able to take more leisurely advantage of marketing-time. But was it still of such importance to us? I mean I must already have moved from Ambert's bed into Jeanne's, and by then concealments would have been a thing of the past. Finally, my future stepmother leaving as much to desire as ever, I did not hesitate to take an heroic decision, that of moving in definitively with my sweetheart and her mother. That didn't even cause a ripple in Courbevoie, moreover. My father had ended up not caring a damn, and as for my future stepmother, she was only too tickled to have achieved her ends. I was even allowed to take a little sewing table that had belonged to my mother, as well as a little Louis XVI wall clock, both of which I transported one evening, on foot, the clock's striking mecha-

nism functioning without interruption the whole way. And so scarcely two months after the retreat from the uncle's house everything had worked out nicely. While Madame Ambert had to some extent lost her son, she'd picked one up in me, and at the same time Jeanne and I had a complete lovelife at last. No strain whatever, it all came about as naturally as can be, and we even gave up saving appearances, which are deceiving anyhow, and for all concerned. We were man and wife, neither more nor less—more, I'd say, rather than less. Jeanne and I had but one bed, Madame Ambert kept house, and when Ambert chanced by for the night, we simply set up a bed for him next to ours. They were halcyon days; a good panorama of them will surely be appreciated. I went each morning to *La République française* and came home each evening. Rue Saint Jacques, Rue Gay-Lussac, Rue Monsieur le Prince, Rue de l'Ancienne Comédie and Rue Mazarine, the Pont des Arts, the Avenue de l'Opéra and La Chaussée d'Antin to number 42—how often I made that trek! I still see their faces, the people I was in the custom of meeting at a given hour, at a given place, unfailingly. Now and then I run into some of them, and they are so changed, so aged, still more so than I, it seems to me. It is thus that at number 57 Rue Monsieur le Prince there was in those days a *brassérie* called Le Boléro, out of which women operated, one of them being a very beautiful girl whom I used to see standing at the threshold whenever I went by. She intrigued me greatly, for I found that she bore a resemblance

49

to one of Jeanne's aunts, the renowned singer. A trifle more bosom, perhaps? The Boléro has disappeared, and that woman, considerably faded today, is now outside another *brassérie,* on the Rue de Vaugirard, very near the Rue Corneille. At least I caught a glimpse of her there when I went by the place not long ago. By six I would be home. There was no running water in the house, and I would go at once to fetch two huge buckets at a little drinking fountain which still exists on the Boulévard de Port Royal, opposite number 113. However, in my memory it used to be a little closer to the corner, and they must have moved it when new buildings were put up. That chore didn't bother me at all, indeed I often made several trips. You feel so fit when you're in love. After dinner, regularly, we went out for a stroll, like everybody else. We would go to the Luxembourg Gardens. Madame Ambert would take a seat on a bench and jabber away with acquaintances she had made, old characters, men and women, of whom every neighborhood has its collection, while Jeanne and I would wander off to bill and coo by ourselves. Or else we'd just go and sit down at the Place de l'Observatoire, at that time still a pleasant spot, without the station or the Garnier of today, with the Closerie des Lilas, then an old café, not showy and ugly as it is now, and the statue of Marshal Ney on the other side, beneath the trees, in front of Bullier, not so glittering either. It was still the Place de l'Observatoire as described in a stanza by Monsier Coppée.* For that matter, the whole of this *quartier* has changed since those days. The Rue Saint Jacques, not yet widened, without the mill-like buildings of the new Sorbonne, was still a picturesque old street for its entire length. The Boulévard Saint Michel itself, the least Parisian part of Paris, still had a little quality it has completely lost thanks to the taverns and the reputedly fashionable dress-shops you see there now. Nor were you deafened, as you are today, by the hideous mechanically propelled tramways and by the underground racket of the trains that go out to Sceaux. Where the Taverne du Panthéon stands you had a big ladies' apparel store, Aux Galéries du Panthéon, which most certainly was not more of an eyesore. There especially, what a change! Nowadays you hardly see anything new in ladies' wear. No, what you see is always the same women. It strikes me also that the Luxembourg was not so full then of this pretentious rabble of up-and-coming painters, with their unsightly wives, who are the reason why I've ceased to set foot there. Finally, the whole area, Luxembourg included, was not encumbered by this profusion of stonework we have to put up with at present, from the starved-looking *Penseur* and those two pharmacists, *Pelletier et Caventou,* to *Le Play* and *Leconte de l'Isle* by way of the *Chopins,* the *Saint Beuves, Angiers,* and assorted *Auguste Comtes.* Yes, all that has changed indeed. To realize how much, I have only to recall the Sundays I had then. What picnics they were, those Sundays! Today, I'd certainly not have the strength for them. You're not young forever. The day comes when you have to settle down. But when I think back on the fun I had, I'm rather proud of myself. On those particular days we left Madame Ambert at home, and that in itself boosted our spirits. Jeanne and I would then set off for the Luxembourg and take several turns around the bandstand, a distraction of which certain people plainly never tire, for to this day through the grillwork I continue to see some who date from that period, and they are still turning. I remember myself well enough, freshly shaven, wearing nothing but black, and Jeanne, on the contrary, in one of her light-colored dresses, with one of her dazzling hats. Or else we'd go and pose for an hour at the Concerts-Rouge, then installed at the corner of the Rue Gay-Lussac and the Boulévard Saint Michel, on the spot where they have put the new Sceaux station, not so noisy, it must be conceded. There I remember seeing a young violinist, seventeen years old at the most, with a delightful face, at whom I stared unwearyingly. After that, dinner. And after dinner, out we went again. I had remained on speaking terms with my father, I had his theater pass every Sunday, and we would go to the Comédie, each time having the same balcony seats, those nearest the stage, second row, right side as you faced the stage. There did my mind take shape enough from listening almost every Sunday, for nigh unto two years, to such quantities of high-flown claptrap, uttered in a manner and in a tone so false and so idiotic, by our well known great artists. With all those shows, fortunately, it was the same as with all those great books I read for such a long while: they served only to reinforce, little by little, my impassioned and exclusive taste for myself. Once, Jeanne wanted to get a closer look at the performing company from within the prompter's box, and my father, having agreed, showed such amiableness toward her, while I was in the audience, that I had a moment of concern. To counterbalance those excesses, why not also include a tender recollection of our own overflowings of the heart in that lone and so narrowly proportioned bedroom, our bed touching the bed of Madame Ambert—did she hear? did she not hear?—Madame Ambert who at any rate never seemed to have heard and never made any allusion to it. So it was that, despite my eighteen years, I already had visions of making love a little differently. Nothing shocking, no perversity (. . . . .) How many other details, other memories! and of all kinds, in connection with this first grand passion. Jeanne's astonishing resemblance to the woman in Chéret's* drawings, then greatly in vogue. The evenings when, spreading all my papers out before me, I used to try to work, without succeeding; no doubt waiting for inspiration, in which I must have believed in those days. I kept my wits about me, though, love notwithstanding. One Sunday Jeanne was pretty ill and obliged to stay in bed. Her moans and groans were a dreadful nuisance, and I could find nothing better than to go out for a walk, and not come back until nightfall. I also remember the popular songs she would sing, without ever

knowing all the lines of any of them. One, whose tune I
still know, began this way:

> *Je ne songeais pas à Rose,*
> *Rose au bois vint avec moi,*
> *Nous parlions de quelque chose,*
> *Moi je ne sais plus de quoi . . .*

And in another, with a richer melody and much more
to the point, there was something like this:

> *Si tu m'aimes, si l'ombre de ma vie . . .*

I can still even hear her way of singing them, the first
one especially, the syllables very distinct, very staccato,
and her voice, a rather low-pitched voice with little ten-
dencies to break, one of those voices that have always
touched me, why yes. Frequently, I remember, she
would amuse herself performing whole series of quite
remarkable splits, like a regular acrobat. And the door-
mats, the milk-boxes she would pick up and move to
another floor in the buildings we went into, and the
apples she'd pinch from fruit-stands! I alluded to that in
Le petit ami, in a passage I wrote about her during the
period of my great despairs. Meanwhile, like her
brother, she had become reacquainted with her father,
had been to Levallois several times, and I ended up
going there too. Ambert had entered upon his higher
destinies. He had left the Ecole des Arts Décoratifs and
was now working with his father, for the same firm on
the Boulévard des Capucines, retouching photographs.

Coincidentally, the idea of going into the theater had occurred to him, and he was preparing seriously for the Conservatory examination, his pockets permanently supplied with paperback masterpieces, out of which he learned solely this or that scene or role, without bothering with the rest, exactly as the boulevard professionals do, that being an excellent way to bring out the whole of the character you are playing. Nor had he neglected his successes with women; he had not completed a year in Levallois before he became the lover of his father's mistress. That delicate story had had a very moving beginning, by the way. Suddenly fallen gravely ill with typhoid fever, Ambert had spent several months in bed at Levallois, nursed with great amicability by his father's mistress, Laure, the only person out of that whole crowd I still see from time to time. Laure was then between thirty and thirty-five, and was still rather pretty; whilst as for Ambert, he was so seductive, so thoroughly what women call a good-looking guy! No distinction, but, better than that, a solid physique and a wonderful way of peering at them that invited to a smashing session in bed. The situation itself had done the rest, and by dint of being there alone together, all day long, for several months, his illness bringing them into close proximity, they had ended up wrapped in each other's legs. The earlier phase of Ambert's convalescence had been one prolonged idyll. Directly his father left in the morning, Ambert would take his place in his bed, and would add further finishing touches to the new conquest achieved through his pretty speeches, his languorous glances, and his interesting looks. Ambert recovered, and the affair went along without his father ever suspecting anything, anymore than he suspected my own affair with his daughter, of which only Laure was aware through what Ambert had told her in confidence. In agreement with their father, Jeanne and Ambert referred to Laure as "Auntie." That simplified everything and got round any awkwardnesses. And let's not forget the pleasure these arrangements insured! Jeanne had found a little job in an embroidery business owned by some Russians on the Boulévard Haussmann. Frequently I would pick her up at Saint Augustin, after my office, and we would go to Levallois to dine with Ambert, with his father, with Laure and Laure's little seven-year-old son, who was Ambert's and Jeanne's half-brother, and sometimes Ambert would accompany us home afterward, just to say hello to his admirable mother. What gay rides they were, the three of us larking on the upper deck of the Panthéon-Place Courcelles omnibus. The evenings we all spent together at Levallois were equally entertaining. After dinner, Ambert and his father discussed art, a specialty of theirs. Monsieur Ambert would hark back to his youth, his former dreams of glory, when he imagined himself following in the footsteps of his opera singer father and vying with his two comic opera singing sisters; and finally, rising in response to his son's entreaty, would break into I know not what roaring song: *Whiter yet than ermine white . . .*

with which he used to bring the house down in days bygone. A plethora of talent fairly choked that man, and he would be forced to go out on the balcony for some fresh air, to pull himself together. And while he was out there, what strings of rapid-fire kisses between Ambert and Laure! Ambert was a mite uncertain about my opinion, at the beginning, and one evening, eager to sound me out, he explained the situation. His father was an artist, his mother had not proven equal to the task; after that, goodbye marriage. Was that not coming from a good son? Not wanting to be outdistanced, I at once replied that I concurred with him, and that I fully understood how his mother could have found herself ditched. Youth is fairly perceptive, sometimes. But my most personal recollection is of a week-day when Jeanne and I went to Levallois for lunch. Ambert and his father were in Paris working. We were alone with Laure and her son. After lunch, it being time for the boy to go back to school, Laure went with him to another room to get him ready, leaving us by ourselves in the dining room for a moment. Jeanne, casting her napkin aside, absolutely had to make love then and there, and without further ado she lay right down on the floor, pulled up her skirts, and loving her didn't take me two minutes ... Poor gorgeous darling, who today is an overweight middle-class housewife and a principled mother of a family. Will she ever read all that I am writing here of that glowing period, and even if she reads it, will she let herself be stirred by it? Ah, along with my youth it's also the whole of hers I am describing!

It does look as though my first love was getting as big a place in this book as she has in my heart. Before proceeding further I ought to say a few words about two friends I was then much involved with. I'd even be willing, in connection with them, to hear the blessings of friendship extolled. For some time I have been looking for the best way to speak about them, I'm still puzzled, and this whole section is apt to be weak. As I like to keep moving along with my work, I'll just go ahead and have a shot at it. Of those two friends one remains to me today, my friend Van Bever, about whom I have spoken before, and he is so accustomed to finding no talent in anyone that I shall cause him no surprise. How I wish I had the time to devote an entire chapter to the friendship that has gone on between us for nearly twenty-five years. I met Van Bever in Courbevoie around 1883, we were the same age, and after I'd lost sight of him for a while I came upon him taking the train into Paris every morning, as I was doing, those being the days when I was still living with my father and traveling with Ambert. At that point Van Bever was already a writer, and I sometimes say to myself that since writing it was to be, I ought to have made up my mind then and benefitted from his example, instead of waiting so long. In this way I would perhaps be as well known as he, which is rather far from the case. To be sure, that still would not have prevented him from being my senior in the career of letters. Note that nothing is more difficult than to not have a senior in literature. No one who writes is able to sing, as in *La Marseillaise,* "We shall enter the career when our elders are no longer there." Quite the contrary, elders are always there, and even forebears: witness Monsieur Catulle Mendès.* As for Van Bever, I know few examples of such literary precociousness. At the age of eleven he was already everything he is today. We went to the same school, he was one grade ahead of me, and he was already writing, and already talking literature, just as well as today. The only difference was in his output. He was concentrated then upon the theater, great grim dramas, which he wrote after school hours, and which he kept secret from his family. What strength that provides, to have found one's way so young! Van Bever was able to switch his line, and devote himself to works of a less harrowing character. The head start he already had on me when we were schoolboys has remained to him, and while I have so far written scarcely two books, his list of *Works by the Same Author* almost forms an entire brochure. At the time when I met up with him again, and he made Ambert's acquaintance, Van Bever's brilliance was finding a temporary outlet in journalism: he was running Courbevoie's local newspaper, in which he was doing his best to demolish the mayor, a worthy pharmacist named Rolland, who, as a matter of fact, went shortly to his grave. At the paper he had become acquainted with a young Lyonnais by the name of Pierre Gaillard, a boy of our age, who had recently come to

Courbevoie to live with an elderly relative. Pierre Gaillard, who died three or four years back after having plunged into what is most inimitable in literature, the Maizeroy or Esparabès* variety, was also a budding writer who had already turned out a verse adaptation of *Faust* and a sizable stock of poetry. A polemicist of Van Bever's class won his esteem at once; whereas he, for having put *Faust* into verse, had seemed to Van Bever a man of his own sort; and they had soon become inseparable friends, spending their time discussing literature, as if that could serve some purpose. Those gentlemen having been presented, the reader is now about to witness the collapse of all that cherished happiness described hereinbefore. "Breaking off is hard when love is at an end," La Rochefoucauld has observed. Jeanne and I still adored each other, and things fell nicely to pieces during the whole of a fine year. I put all I possibly could into it, circumstances also contributed their share, and Van Bever and Gaillard helped out too, albeit unwittingly, for I had not confided in either one. Suddenly gripped by an overpowering thirst for freedom, I began by resigning my job at *La République française,* a fine start in as much as I had no other livelihood. That happened, I believe, around June or July of 1890. Seeing I had become free, Van Bever resolved to bring me together with Gaillard, who more and more seemed to him an extraordinary fellow, marked out for the greatest future. Parenthetically, it is unimaginable, the number of persons Van Bever introduced me to over a ten-year

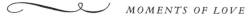

period, under this pretext that they were marked out for the greatest future in the different branches of art, and who subsequently wound up as ordinary shopkeepers or small-town employees. He would arrive one day, all aboil, would tell me about so-and-so, a remarkable chap, whom I absolutely had to get to know. So either he would bring his protégé to see me or I'd go to see him, and a week later there Van Bever would be, telling me just as heatedly that the same so-and-so was beyond question an out-and-out cretin, at best fit to rot in a scullery. And so acquaintance with Gaillard was placed on the agenda, and Ambert being invited too, we both betook ourselves to Courbevoie. It was truly a magnificent day, in that little salon on the Rue Carle Hébert, where the household chickens wandered about pecking and stinking, altogether at home. With his elderly relative in the chair, and before the three of us who listened to him with the air of so many experts, Ambert with respect to elocution, Van Bever with respect to scenic qualities, and I with respect to subtlety of feeling, Gaillard read his *Faust,* five acts, and the final line delivered, there followed an hour-long concert of admiration and felicitations. Ambert, especially, would not subside, already seeing himself in the role of Faust, assuring us all he would create a sensation, complaining however that the play lacked women. A huge meal ensued, in Van Bever's private quarters adjoining the quay, and it was not until morning that the party broke up. How otherwise than that such high pleasures be repeated? Jeanne was still in her embroidery shop, leaving early and returning late, and she was now the one who longed to be at home. Meanwhile I was loafing about or going to play the dilettante alongside my friends, just like someone on an annuity. Happy friends, you to whom I gave so much of my life in those days, to the detriment of my perfect love, which little by little slipped away without giving me warning. Oh, the literary discussions I listened to between Van Bever and Gaillard in Courbevoie. I also went to Levallois to listen to Ambert rant from sun-up to sun-down, in view of the approaching Conservatory examination, despite which he repeated incessantly that with his endowments, he could just as well tackle the examination in voice. Everybody else was working, I alone was without an objective. Theater and literature interested me too, but I took no step toward them, was incapable of the slightest effort, preferring, during moments of quiet, to sleep as much as possible. What a sleeper I was then! It could be in any bed, and I would easily have slept for a week; it was the finest use I put my time to when I wasn't off with my friends, or else heading for Paris, wild as I always was about those excursions. However, I do believe there was a moment when I had a brief inclination to apply to the Conservatory, like Ambert. Talent's stimulating influence, presumably. It's so infectious, when one is young, to hear someone vociferate, the while gesticulating, after the fashion of our nation's foremost actors. Once every week also Van Bever and I had a standing rendezvous at the corner of the Boulévard Saint Michel and the Rue Soufflot, and we would explore the literary scene thoroughly. His undertakings were steadily broadening, tragedies, vaudeville, comedies, short stories, lectures and newspaper articles, all needing nothing further than to go to press. Always up there ahead, as I pointed out, and his hours unceasingly devoted to toiling for glory.

Then, at the end of the year, a major change. I don't know why it was, but since I'd been living more with her, Madame Ambert had become more admirable than before, and as frankness is the privilege of youth and I was beginning to tire of having all these people nagging me, I told the big lady pretty much what I thought of her exceptional lack of mental gifts. Whereupon there was such wailing—which instead of melting me, only made me twit her the more—that I decided, despite Jeanne's supplications and tears, to go live by myself, alone, and truly under my own roof. Well, Madame Ambert herself was of a mind to move. Everybody would change surroundings at the same time. Accompanied by Jeanne, I consequently hunted for a room, and I soon chose a large one on the sixth floor at 14 Rue Monsieur le Prince, while Madame Ambert picked for herself and her daughter an apartment on the Rue Saint Jacques, almost at the corner it forms with the Rue Gay-Lussac, next to a sort of convent which still exists. All that transpired in January of 1891. At its Boulévard Saint Michel end, the Rue Monsieur le Prince, instead of the iron railings you see there now, had the old wooden railings such as they appear in the illustrations of *Les Rois en exil*. I had found a little job at *Le Siècle,* a newspaper whose offices were on the Rue Chauchat, with the option of going there when I wanted, and I began a new existence that I'll describe very rapidly, skipping, regretfully, a good many details. For example, the inauguration of my new bed: the delivery man who brought it was no sooner gone than Jeanne insisted upon proceeding to that pleasure forthwith. Or what she did to get me in form that evening when, stretched upon her back and naked (. . . . .) I lose the calm great writing demands, whenever I remember those things. It was in that room I made my entrance into literature, to the tune of at least one hundred lines of verse a day that flowed from an inspiration without bounds, on the whole, and which, the entire stack of them, were torn up when I left the Rue Monsieur le Prince. Despite his talent, Ambert had failed to get into the Conservatory, and was retouching photographs again, now for an employer in the Rue Cadet area. Levallois was no more. Monsieur Ambert had finally noticed that Laure was betraying him with his son; or was it that he, a great womanizer also, had fallen violently in love with another mistress, for example the one with whom he is living today—with whom they are both living, perhaps? But one fine morning he didn't come home, once again leaving a woman and a child in the lurch, disappearing without being found or heard from again. Fortunately

for Laure, Ambert was a gallant young man, who also knew how to combine the useful with the agreeable. He addressed a lengthy reprimand to his mother, who probably understood not one word of it. Laure turned up, the two women embraced each other in their common distress, and a month later Laure and her son came to live on the Rue Saint Jacques, a few doors down the street from Madame Ambert. In the daytime everybody lived as one family, the ex-wife, the ex-mistress and the lover-son, and in the evening Ambert and Laure went home together, like a Romeo and a Juliette. As for Jeanne and myself, we stuck to our little routines. No great shakes. We spent evenings with one another, and every Saturday night she would come to my room, we would have a workout, then stay together until the following evening. I must add that I did my best to vary the program. Often on Sunday morning I would receive a telegram from Gaillard, saying he was expecting me in Courbevoie with Van Bever, and with that I'd up and go, undeterred by her complaints that instead of a nice day of snuggling she was about to have to return to her mother's. The unspoken thoughts she must have had during that period, secretly nourished by Laure and Ambert, who seized every opportunity to steer her away from her affair—pretty girl that she was, and who would have so little trouble managing on her own! Yes, my stock had definitely started to fall, and it wasn't because of less love but simply because time was passing, and because life beckoned—and because she wanted to live.

Well, those lofty matters escaped me. My understanding them, furthermore, would probably have made no difference. In no time at all my character had completely changed. My mind was on nothing but writing, living, and dreaming. Loving came afterward. The remaining vestiges of our intimacy . . . I even went so far as to sacrifice it to friendship, careless of all pleasure save my own. It was in fact at this juncture that Van Bever shared my lodgings for a time, from about May until July. Jeanne got scarcely anything beyond Saturdays, when I would pack Van Bever off to sleep somewhere else, tidying the place up for our amours, plus a Sunday now and then, when my great-men-to-be weren't demanding my presence in Courbevoie. And on that subject too, what must her thoughts have been! As I never found out exactly, I feel I might give a few brief details touching my existence with Van Bever during those two months. The rest will be for later on, when I will do a literary study of my own on myself, which is still the best way of having things right. Van Bever has a clear memory of his arrival at the Rue Monsieur le Prince one evening towards six o'clock. I wasn't in, and to find me he had to go to a little grocery, at number 26 on the same street, where I sometimes took my meals. The grocer, it seems, was in the midst of asking me what a *chose béante* could be. Van Bever, whose knowledge of the French language was already vast, at once broke into the conversation. "A *chose béante?* Why," said he, "something that gapes is something deep." But the

grocer was not convinced, little aware that he was deal-
ing with a powerful opponent. "All right," he said to
Van Bever, "let's look it up in the dictionary!" and the
discussion went on between them until I finished dinner. One can have no conception of the books and
papers Van Bever was accompanied by, complete works
of Voltaire, of Rollin, Villemain, Millevoye, La Harpe,
etc., with the manuscripts of his own works, also complete. I already loathed accumulations of books and
papers, and once he arrived upon my territory, the very
first thing I did, his protests notwithstanding, was toss
the whole kit and caboodle methodically out of the
window. In the morning those literatures were carpet-
ing the pavement, which brought on some speeches
from the concierge. After that the two months passed
by without anything special happening. Towards one
o'clock every day we would emerge and proceed gravely
to a little restaurant in the Rue de l'Ancienne Comédie,
where we consumed much hot chocolate, up to seven or
eight cups, sometimes. The lunch hour was over, and
we had all the personnel to ourselves. We tried to obtain credit there one day, it was refused with great
promptness. Next, Van Bever would drag me along to
the quays, to poke for hours in the booksellers' stalls
while I waited for him, never having had the taste or
patience for that, and we would head back laden with
books, which after they had been looked through, had
to be exchanged or resold. We also spent lots of time
under the Odéon arcades, keeping abreast. I've just

stopped and spent a good quarter of an hour deliberating. After all, why not come out with it, whatever the reaction of "honest, upstanding people." A great frenzy of reading had taken possession of me, an immense curiosity, a desire to discover everything, know everything; about this wonderful lines have been written. Only, I wasn't swimming in wealth. And something else I have never been able to stand is the reading room crowd in public libraries. So when the need for a book became too much for me, I'd swipe it. There. That happened two or three times. Thus, one day, having leafed through *The Life of Jesus* in the sixty-centimes edition, I was unable to restrain myself and left the arcades with the volume in my pocket, in order to read it at my leisure at home, to the great indignation of Van Bever, who did not fancy that kind of literature, he told me. In the evening, in my room, we spent our time drinking coffee, cup after cup, Van Bever smoking an enormous pipe with a bowl carved to look like Voltaire, and by midnight we were in such high fettle that we would go out and walk I don't know how many times around the Luxembourg Gardens before retiring. Whenever I had a little money I would do Van Bever a kindness, always the same one. I would conduct him to a hairdresser's and there, despite his protests, directing the barber to lay hold of him, would order his hair to be cut, lots of it. Very often did I thus spend my last sou. The amount removed was always insufficient. To obtain a result it would have been necessary to make the rounds in a given day of all the hairdressers in the neighborhood. Indeed, we vied fiercely with one another in sartorial elegance. Van Bever then owned a pair of black and white checked trousers, whose pattern he would touch up every morning with the aid of a brush and two little cakes of watercolor paint, which over the course of time had given that garment a rather British stiffness. As for me, so fastidious in the article of footwear, I dare say I have never been better shod than I was then, with an admirable pair of Molière-type slippers with silver buckles, which my father had worn when he played repertory, and which I'd been allowed to take from the house on one of his generous days.

On the floor below my room lived some sort of old rentier named Guérin with whom we were on good terms. He had coveted an old shotgun I had in my room, I'd given it to him, and from time to time he invited us to lunch. When he went too long without remembering this obligation, Van Bever would remind him of it by leaning out the window and shouting to him. We always found him at home in the company of a little squirt of more than effeminate demeanor, his nephew so-called but far more probably a catamite, or whatever, the sharer of his intimate delights. I still encounter this phenomenon fairly often in the vicinity of the Gare Montparnasse, always toddling along with the same little steps, bottom wiggling like a young tart's. A room adjoining mine was occupied by a young house-maid, a rather pretty creature, whom Van Bever was courting. As we were coming in one evening, he thought he recognized, in a woman climbing the stairs ahead of us, the tender object of his passion. He leapt forward, caught her round the waist, he was about to embrace her when the woman, turning in his direction, to his kiss offered the face of the concierge in person, gasping from astonishment. From that day on Van Bever was known in the house as a chap who runs after women, the concierge beholding him with the incensed gaze of jealousy, whilst our neighbor, disenchanted, was unwilling to listen to any more of his declarations.

I also remember Van Bever's pitying attitude toward the poetry I was turning out with such fervor. He had glanced at it once or twice; already endowed with a great critical sense, he told me frankly one day that I was not at all cut out for literature, and that I would do best to give it up. They of course abound with advice who have nothing at stake. Jeanne had got to know him little by little, and when she and I were going every Tuesday—among connoisseurs, *the* day to go—to the Théâtre Montparnasse, where I had obtained tickets through the director, Monsieur Hartmann, an old friend of my father, Van Bever would be with us. There one night we even reached an agreement with Monsieur Paul Albert, Hartmann's associate, over a piece of light comedy that we were to write jointly, an ambitious project of which nothing came. How happy Van Bever is going to be to relive all that in the pages of a book. I have tried talking to him about it, on occasion, but emotion so takes hold of him that conversation is impossible.

And now two words, in passing, about a voluntary misfire that dates from this time, the one-night stand with Gaillard's sister, then in her thirties, an exceedingly dark young woman newly arrived from her native province, and upon whom I had made a certain impact, it must be supposed. For was she not induced to challenge me to spend a night next to a woman without touching her, generously offering herself for this experiment? She altogether misjudged me, whether it was for a simpleton or a cad. The experiment was carried out in the same Hotel de Lisbonne mentioned earlier, and she was able to leave me the next morning without my even having kissed her. See to it you are tactful with women! Had I jumped her, she would have acted outraged, and for simply having kept my word, the young lady called me every name under the sun.

Late in June Van Bever left me; and Jeanne and I had a few days of intimacy once again, full of the ripeness that foreshadows the end. And it was approaching indeed. Yet another year of amours, on the sly and by appointment, and then it would be the final kiss-off. I continued to be so short of money, *Le Siècle* soon firing me for never showing up. Finally there was no way of keeping on in business. My father, for his part, was urging me to enlist, assuring me that I was mistaken in thinking I could avoid military service thanks to my near-sightedness, and making all sorts of promises about

71

the things he would do for me. Jeanne, whom I con-
sulted, said nothing one way or another, except that,
after all, we would not be farther apart; and so, poorly
supported by her, who had made her own plans, and
without any energy of my own, I ended by giving in. I
shall not dwell upon my father's pretty behavior toward
me in this connection. After having spoken so highly of
him there is no need for me to bury him under a heap of
rhetorical flowers. The flowers adorning the gracious
garden where he reposes ought to suffice. When at last I
finally agreed I was invited to return to his house, and I
left the Rue Monsieur le Prince. That was in the closing
days of July or the first ones of August. Jeanne, as it
happened, had just rented a room at 7 Rue des Feuillantines, simply to have more freedom away from her
mother, she explained to me, and she hastened to have
my furniture transported there. My little darling was
preparing one of those mighty surprises for me! who
hadn't the faintest idea what was coming, decidedly not.
In Courbevoie they were getting ready to doublecross
me too, and from my future stepmother I later learned
how my father had urged her to take good care of me,
begrudging me nothing, so as to turn me back into a
sturdy lad again, sure to be found fit for service. The
good man was toying with the idea of getting rid of me
by sending me off to drill-fields in the provinces somewhere, Montargis, I believe. He already had it all fixed
up. But one evening, as I was talking with him about it,
he blundered into revealing that the promises he had

made me in front of witnesses were false, and so that did it, both with regard to his scheme and to my villeggiatura, for I was given a day to leave the premises. However, I had to find somewhere else to go. Go back with Jeanne? I can no longer recall whether it even crossed my mind. Since my return to my father's house I had been seeing Gaillard nearly every day. I told him what was up. He knew the commanding officer of a light infantry battalion garrisoned at Courbevoie itself. Gaillard spoke to him about me. It was agreed that the major would examine me only for the sake of form. I took the necessary steps, and on October 20, 1891, at ten p.m., I made my entrance into the Courbevoie barracks, signed up for three years.

I shall not say a very great deal about the seven months I spent in uniform before discarding it forever. I was never much amused by barracks tales, even in the books of Monsieur Courteline,* which bored me, actually. For captain I had a worthy drunkard, whose military capacity went no farther than the troops' clothing store, and who one day saved me from pretty serious trouble for having voiced my opinion on periods of extra duty. Neither do I wish to forget Captain Walsin Esterhazy,* so famous since the Dreyfus Affair, and who was our battalion adjutant. I can see him now, on inspection days when all the officers collect in the courtyard around the major, Esterhazy standing a little apart from everyone else, haughty and disdainful. Once I underwent an examination before him following my request to be removed from among those considered for promotion, on account of poor eyesight and inadequate health, and I have rarely seen an officer so charming, natural and polite. Along with Garrison Adjutant Moty, of whom I shall speak later, those comprise all my good memories from soldiering days. Let me add that I didn't care a fig about becoming a general. Passes were my sole preoccupation. I regularly had one every Saturday evening until midnight on Sunday. There was one time, at Christmas, when, as I had been punished, I did not get the pass I had counted upon. Three days to spend in Paris with Jeanne! I decided to kill myself. I had already cocked my rifle, and I was sitting on my cot when one of the men came up, snatched my gun away, and went to notify the captain. What a fine gathering of officers around me for the next half-hour! They eagerly awarded me an extended leave up until New Year's. Did I really intend to kill myself, would I really have pulled the trigger? Perhaps! I no longer know. I was so romantic, you see, and that barracks, with its brutes of all kinds, was so little to my liking! However, trying now to recapture my feelings at the time, that can hardly have been anything else than pure make-believe.

And during this period what beautiful turns my love affair was taking! Laure's and Ambert's advice had indeed been heard, and was shortly acted upon, especially the advice offered by Laure, who was urging her "niece" to go into the theater, where, Laure told her, she could easily find a reliable keeper, all the while hanging on to me if she was so inclined. My dear Jeanne was now in lavishly staged reviews, and sounded just like everybody else singing in the chorus-line, dressed in the least complicated costumes possible. She had perhaps sensed the artist in herself, she too, and I had become, without changing, the lover of an actress, the dream of so many young men. Why is it, when one loves, that everything must change? I had a first inkling of something exactly one day after I entered the army: that was when I heard the news from Madame Ambert, always the first when it came to spilling the beans. At the outset I failed to see the agreeable side to these developments, responding only with a silly feeling of jealousy and grief. Had I but known as well, as I was soon to find out, that I had been promoted also to the rank of *fancy man!* Ah, I would have done the same, certainly, I would have resigned myself to my good fortune. Jeanne remained so charming with me, did indeed "hang on" to me so well, that her outpourings of warmth took the chill out of me. We would meet every Saturday night after her show got out, and go back together to the Rue des Feuillantines. Our fine sessions of love-making in that room, back in full form as I was—my sole military glory! The theater would tie her up the next day, which I would spend there in her room until evening, and then return to Courbevoie and my life amid the savages. I see it well, that room whose windows looked out upon the Val-de-Grâce courtyards, and Van Bever must remember it too from all the times he came to pass away the afternoon with me. Then, at the barracks, they sent me to Val-de-Grâce. It was the end of February. Jeanne and I had to make do with visits. They were on Thursdays, and she would spend them cracking jokes about my enforced chastity, and, when we found ourselves alone in a corridor, letting me have a peep at her breasts (. . . .) And her solicitude didn't stop there. She wrote to me and sent me money. So I was being a bit kept too, and that money certainly came from the beloved Clozel, the reliable keeper to whom I am about to come. That's a kind of revenge too, after all. Otherwise, my life as an invalid wasn't all that bad. On Sundays I would have visits from Laure and Madame Ambert, and sometimes from Van Bever as well. Even my amiable father came once, at two fifty-five, which ruled out any eventual effusions, visits ending at three o'clock. The rest of the time I acted as secretary to the medical officer in my ward, Doctor Moty, for his professional reports, or I idled the time away with two or three of the better quality patients, or I listened to the whole ward bellow forth the latest tunes in chorus. Does it not date from this period, February to May of 1892, the song that contains these extraordinary lines:

> *Il est en or, il est en or,*
> *On dirait qu'il prend son essor,*
> *C'n'est pas du toc, ni du melchior,*
> *Comm' la cann' du tambour-major,*
> *Il est en or, il est en or*

—when you've heard that for three months, day after heroic day, its beauty is engraved in your mind for the rest of your life.

It was then that after the example of other patients like myself I made bold to ask the medical officer for a pass. It was a Thursday afternoon in early April. I had got word to Jeanne and she was waiting for me. That afternoon was truly one of the high points in our affair. After a few pleasures, and once straightened out and spiffy again, as I was hanging about waiting for her to get herself dressed, I noticed on the mantelpiece a photograph of some third-rate comedian with a knucklehead grin, and he looked to be nearing forty. An oversight on Jeanne's part, probably. It's so difficult for women to think of everything. Questioning her upon the quality of this young fellow thus enthroned in her abode, I at first obtained information of only trifling importance, delivered in a studiously negligent tone. Somebody in the troupe, one of the bunch from the theater, an artist, that is, nothing at all. She handled it so skillfully that this time I was suspicious. Had she got anywhere, I asked her, with that halfbaked lie of hers? As one always says in such cases, wasn't it better that I know? Better, yes, so much so that Jeanne decided to open up her heart to me. That photograph, I learned then, was of Paul Clozel, the star of her theater, a buffoon fairly well known for his eunuch's voice and his pot belly, and for the past several months her reliable keeper into the bargain. Ah, all these things, which I have condensed, and not enough at that, and about which I have since absolutely ceased to care, what pain they caused me that day, sitting without a word on a little chair between the fireplace and the window. Dressed in a military outfit though I was, mine was not a martial appearance. Jeanne had expected a scene, probably, and she couldn't get over my silence. All the while going ahead with her dressing, she lavished kind words upon me, words most comforting, and told me the whys and wherefores of her new idyll. Clozel had been so good to her when she entered the theater, advice, attentions, etc. And he had continued to act like a father, and what a father! giving her everything she needed, coming from time to time to sleep with her in the morning. He was married, that meant he had to be careful. But his wife was a bitch (naturally) and he was going to get a divorce, then he'd marry her. She even advanced the excuse that he looked like me, had the same first name! What was at stake was his position, she added, and I ought to understand, if I loved her. Besides, was she saying anything about not seeing each other anymore? It would be a little less often, and being careful, that's all. Great happiness as available as ever, yet despite that I felt no better. It was magnificent, all she was telling me. A love built upon goodness! What luxury compared to the way in which acquaintances are ordinarily struck up in the wings. An actor espies a woman, someone in the chorus or a walk-on, feels he wouldn't mind going to bed with her once, maybe a

couple of times, depending how much of her her costume leaves uncovered. He lays hands upon her breasts or other parts, employing the familiar *tu* at once, and the affair is launched. Clozel, however, was sophisticated big daddy, one piece of clownery on top of others. You also have a pretty keen visual sense at such moments. I could see Clozel, performing the aforesaid gesture; and that adding itself to the idea that he came here to sleep, to lie in my own bed, and as did I . . . ah! perhaps even better than I did . . . Then, ready to go, Jeanne came over to me, took my face in her hands, kissed me, and, supreme consolation, brought out the following speech, which she had perhaps read somewhere, who knows? "Pooh!" she exclaimed, "all the great poets have had an unhappy passion. It'll make you work." Admirable creature, who thus, long before I did, discerned the great literary future that lay ahead of me! Was she absolutely set on alexandrines, though? Except for the great poet part, I shall have done my best, and I do not very well see how, after that speech, she can be vexed with me for relating our amours.

At the conclusion of that scene Jeanne went off to a rendezvous with Clozel, while I went back to the hospital. I shall pass over the uproarious reception I received for returning with such a cheerful countenance. If those ailing gentlemen thought I was in a mood for merriment, they were mistaken. The entire life I was leading had suddenly become still more unbearable, to begin with owing to them, then because of the thought of re-

turning one day or another to the folks in Courbevoie.
Three years of this life, and only six months of it done!
No. No. Or at least I had to give it a try, thanks to the
means I now knew I had for getting myself dismissed,
and I felt a splendid upsurge of determination and energy, my first, which goes to show that one is never
cuckolded without gaining something thereby. I re-
quested an interview with Doctor Moty, who granted it
at once. I discussed my situation, the serious one, need-
less to say, approaching it all from the military view-
point, the uselessness of my enlistment, no rank ahead
of me, three years thrown away, etc., everything that
was not of the slightest importance to me. I can still see
the excellent man listening to me, with his fine bearded
face, his long hair, even less military looking than I. He
must have taken a shine to me, indeed yes, or I must
have spoken very well—the voice of love!—for he cut
me short before long. "I gather you want to be discharged," he said. By way of answer I said neither yes
nor no, remained vague so as not to commit myself,
trusting to my physiognomy. "All right," he resumed,
"we'll take care of it." It was taken care of, all right. I
paid a visit to the battalion eye-doctor who immediately
provided me with the necessary document. Next, Doctor Moty checked me for palpitations, and I was in such
wonderful condition, after all my woes of the heart, that
his verdict was just as swift. There was nothing left for
me to do but calmly wait for the appropriate board to
meet. What might I have complained about? I was

about as heartsore as you can get, and the treatment Jeanne was giving me was the more effective now that I knew where the money came from. Every morning I stood outside her window and waited for her to appear, and when I failed to see her, and the window remained shuttered, I knew what that meant. Clozel was there, and my lovely friend, busy securing her position, was dancing a jig for him. And Jeanne was right in foreseeing the good that would accrue from my sufferings. I had already started working again, spending my afternoons venting my sorrow in little poems, or in little pages of prose, which I managed to write on my bedside table, in the midst of the racket in the ward. A shame I didn't get a picture taken of myself as hospital poet, with my flowing nightgown, my cotton nightcap, and my sickly mien; it would have made a nice item for my iconography. The 14th of May arrived at last. I took my place in a truck alongside other invalids. The Rue Saint Dominique! It was noon. By three o'clock I was back without having seen a single member of the board, but discharged withal. The lot of us, completely naked, had been herded into a small room. At a given moment, from an adjoining room there had come a shout: "Léautaud!" I had shouted "Present!" in response. Thereupon another shout: "Discharged!" In those three words the whole ceremony had been disposed of. Another two or three days for the formalities, and I would re-enter civilian life. I advised Jeanne, who replied that she would be waiting for me, and once I was out I dashed to her place. Ah, that was a better afternoon, that one, with its program of ardor, of caresses, and of melancholy. For, truth to tell, I was not consoled. Despair on such a scale, all in the space of a month! But a free man once more, my immediate happiness made me a little less sensitive to the Clozel business, not so regrettable if looked at pragmatically, and moreover Jeanne was really makings things hum in our attempt to catch up! Too bad that Clozel couldn't have been there, if only in the interests of his art. He would certainly have found it the occasion for something new in wry faces.

By the end of the same day I was under the paternal roof again, and if that made anyone happy beyond words, it was not my father, a great armchair patriot who was thunderstruck by the news of my discharge: "To have a son who is not capable of being a soldier!" he said in a stricken voice. However, as I was still a minor, he was obliged to adapt to the situation and let me have a place to sleep, and I started living again. Three days later, once again cleanshaven and with the hair on my head beginning to grow back, all trace was gone of my passage through the armed forces. At first I was concerned with nothing but Jeanne, that is, with seeing her and with racking my brains thinking about all our difficulties. That poor Clozel deserved pity also, of course. As soon as Jeanne saw herself rid of him for a day she would let me know, and I would arrive to spend it with her. We also had frequent night-time rendez-vous, around twelve-thirty, at the stop where she got off

the trolley returning from the theater, on the corner of
the Rue de l'Abbé de l'Epée and the Boulévard Saint
Michel, and we would stay together until the following
morning. I even went several times to that theater of
theirs, with tickets got from Clozel, and I can see her
now, such a pretty creature in her showy costumes,
against spectacular settings, under dazzling lights, and I
can still hear the tunes sung by the wonderful choruses
she was part of, and I also see Clozel himself, dripping
sweat as he went through his contortions. If ever four or
five days went by without a rendezvous, I'd take things
graciously into my own hands by going and posting
myself in the shadows on the Rue de l'Abbé de l'Epée
until I could surprise Jeanne as she stepped off her trolley. Often Jeanne was accompanied by Clozel, who
would then turn around and go home, obliged to be
forever careful because of his wife. I would see them say
goodbye, kiss each other, then see Clozel go off and
Jeanne start in my direction. "Why, it's you!" she'd say
upon finding me there. "Good gracious, yes!" I would
reply, and we would go to bed together once again. I remember that one morning Clozel turned up while I was
still there. He knocked several times and the two of us
held still until he went away, imagining there was no
one at home. I would also spy on the two of them when
the theater was out. They would go and sit awhile in a
Boulévard Sébastopol café which in the rear gives upon
the Rue Palestro, always taking a table on that side in
order to be less conspicuous, and I would watch them

from outside, through the windows, hidden from their sight by the interior drapes. Ah, what a hand-me-down Othello I made. This whole business lasted a little less than a month, then, her pregnancy advancing, and the theater having closed for the summer, Jeanne left the Rue des Feuillantines and went to live for a time somewhere in the country, not far from Paris, with Clozel. Our amours were over, those treasured amours that I have related with such care, if I am not mistaken. They were to revive for a few months the following year, and could have been revived yet again, had I been more clever. Of Jeanne and of that whole period I preserved a good many little mementoes. First there is the photograph with the dedication I spoke of, and another, very small, that I always carried with me in the earliest stages of our affair, then another, taken at her father's in Levallois, where she is dressed as a man, wearing my clothes and Ambert's beret, then some others from the days of our Faubourg Saint Jacques ménage, and still one more, at the outset of her hook-up with Clozel. In addition I have some ribbons she tied her braids with, and even a little lock, or tuft, of private hair that she gave me one day out of fun, to cheer me up, sometime during our later get-togethers, the lot contained in a little card case which also came from her. But there's a perspective to be maintained here. I held on to all those things somewhat without intending to. Everybody has treasures like these. You put them in a cupboard and don't think about them again. When you change address you come upon them while packing. "I must throw that stuff out," you tell yourself, considering the new surroundings you are moving into. But just then you are in a hurry, too tired, and everything is tucked back into place in a new cupboard. That often continues your whole life long. Which is quite all right so long as you don't involve yourself this way in telling the story of your amours, for then those relics can no longer be got rid of: they form a part of the original manuscript. I also have some letters from her, those she wrote to me at Val-de-Grâce, in connection with her visits or when she sent me money, then at Courbevoie when I was back at my father's again, to let me know she was free and to come quick! then the next to last, when we had her departure with Clozel and the impossibility of our continuing to see each other, and which she wrote to inform me thereof, and to tell me it was goodbye, and to be happy, and to try to forget. I have just reread it, that letter. A pencilled note, in my handwriting, indicates that I received it on the seventh day of June, 1892, at nine o'clock in the evening, and I do indeed have an image of myself going to meet the postman coming up the front path through our garden, and opening that letter right away. How I suffered, reading it; how I went straight up to my room, in order to cry undisturbed. It seems to me, even, that the pain is still there, for all I have to do is remember ... and if I didn't keep tight hold ... Ha. So they're not kidding when they say that we remain sensitive about these things forever, and that in that old heart of ours a place is set aside for them forever, a good place? But what is it to me, actually, this whole story, or even that part of my youth represented in it. I have always lived in a forward direction, and despite this craze I have for writing down what I remember from the past, I am still the same today. Perhaps it's only the idea of the days already amassed behind me, or the secret taste for sadness that I have never lost? A last letter from Jeanne, dated the 12th of the same month of June, proposing a rendezvous at her mother's the following evening—but I have no recollection of that one. One more or one less—true enough, it hardly matters!

1906.

NOTES

page 9 Léautaud's fictional autobiography is made up of three separate but interconnected and complementary works. The first, *Le petit ami,* which appeared in 1903, centers upon his relationship with his mother. In 1905 there followed *In memoriam,* where his father is the central figure. *Moments of Love,* originally published under the title *Amours,* belongs to the year 1906.

page 10 From earliest childhood until about the age of ten Léautaud lived in Paris with his father at an address on the Rue des Martyrs. The child, whose actress mother had abandoned him when he was an infant, was looked after by a nurse he adored.

page 37 In *In memoriam.*

page 39 After General Georges Boulanger (1837–1891), French would-be Napoleon and military dictator, who first distinguished himself in actions in North Africa and Indochina and then at home, in 1871, when he

89

contributed heavily to the crushing of the Paris Commune. Minister of War in 1886, he became the popular hero of an anti-Republican nationalist movement and in 1889 seemed about to take the country over through a *coup d'état*. Instead, he lost his nerve and fled to Belgium; there, on the grave of his mistress, he committed suicide in 1891.

page 39   Joseph Reinach (1856–1921), politician and publicist, campaigned in the press against Boulangism and in support of Dreyfus.

page 39   Jules Ferry (1832–1893), journalist and politician, rose to prominence as Minister of Public Instruction, and was twice premier. Ferry established the modern French educational system with universal, free, and compulsory education in the primary schools. Ferry is also—and perhaps even better—known as one of the most dedicated builders of the French colonial empire.

page 40   Arsène-Arnaud Claretie (1840–1913), "a prolific, versatile, glib but not profound journalist. Man of letters, critic and chronicler whose twenty volumes of *La Vie à Paris* cover the years from 1881 to 1911. His *Portraits contemporains* (1873–5) are popular biography" (*The Oxford Companion to French Literature*).

page 50   François Coppée (1842–1908), "poet and dramatist, born in Paris, was called the 'poète des humbles' be-

cause he wrote about humble people whose drab exteriors might conceal pitiful romances or tragedies. His work has been accused of banality but it had great popular appeal. In later life Coppée became a fervent Roman Catholic and wrote a novel of religious experience _La Bonne Souffrance._ During the Dreyfus case he was prominent in connexion with the notoriously diehard and anti-Semitic _Ligue de la patrie française"_ (_The Oxford Companion to French Literature_).

page 53   The French painter Jules Chéret (1836–1932) has been called the originator of the modern poster.

page 59   Catulle Mendès (1842–1909), Parnassian poet, also novelist, playwright, and man of letters.

page 60   Maizeroy and Esparbès were contemporary authors of patriotic and historical novels, forgotten today.

page 73   Georges Courteline (1861–1929), widely read in his day, specialized in farcical sketches of military life and in satirical sketches of bureaucrats at work.

page 73   Ferdinand Walsin Esterhazy (1847–1923), "French army officer claiming membership in the old Hungarian family of Esterhazy. An adventurer, he had served in the papal army and the French Foreign Legion before entering the regular French army, where he rose to be a major. Deep in debt, he sold French military secrets to the Germans. When evidence of treason leaked out in 1894, the guilt was pinned on Captain Dreyfus. Esterhazy was tried in 1898 upon the insistence of the pro-Dreyfus party, but his fellow officers, still refusing to admit a judicial error, acquitted him. He was later dismissed from the army" (*The Columbia Encyclopedia*).

The design of this book is the work of Marjorie Merena,
of Brattleboro, Vermont. The typesetting has been by
American-Stratford Graphic Services, Inc.,
also of Brattleboro. The printing and binding are by
Northlight Studio Press, of Barre, Vermont.